D1265507

THE NIGHT RIDE

by

AINGELDA ARDIZZONE

Illustrated by

EDWARD ARDIZZONE

Windmill Books AND E. P. Dutton
New York

To my five children

First published in the U.S.A. 1975
by Windmill Books and E. P. Dutton
First published in Great Britain 1973
by Longman Young Books

Published by Windmill Books and E. P. Dutton & Co.
201 Park Avenue South, New York, New York 10003

Library of Congress Cataloging in Publication Data
Ardizzone, Aingelda. The night ride.
SUMMARY: Three discarded toys decide to look
for a new home.
1. Toys—Fiction I. Ardizzone, Edward. II. Title.
PZ8.9.A7Ni4 [E] 75-6743 ISBN 0-525-61535-0
Printed in the U.S.A. First Edition
10 9 8 7 6 5 4 3 2 1

Dandy, Kate and Tiny Teddy had lain forgotten in a dark cupboard for a long time. The children they belonged to had grown up and no longer played with them.

Then, one day just before Christmas, they were taken out of the cupboard and thrown into the dustbin.

Night came and it was dark and uncomfortable in the dustbin. But at dawn a chink of light shone through the gap between the bin and the lid.

The toys gazed sadly around them and wondered how they could get out.

Then Kate saw an old dish-mop. Dand found a broken umbrella and Tiny Teddy

wooden spoon with a very long handle. Together they jumped up and down and pushed the lid off the dustbin. It fell off with a tremendous clatter.

Dandy lifted Tiny Teddy up. He climbed onto the edge of the bin and wriggled out. He slid down to the ground and waited by some flower-pots.

Then Kate and Dandy jumped out of the bin and they all ran away as fast as they could up one road and down another until they found themselves in the country.

They rested for a while and then began to look around. In the hedge behind them they

found an old toy engine. It was rusty here and there where the paint had worn off but the wheels were still strong.

The toys were very excited. They set to work at once to pull the engine out of the hedge. This was not too difficult once they had cleared the

leaves and long grass that had grown up around it.

The toys leapt onto the engine. “I’ll be the driver,” said Dandy, buttoning up his jacket. “We will look for somewhere to live.”

The engine started to move very slowly and then it began to go faster and faster down the road.

Darkness fell but the toys were enjoying the ride so much that they did not want to stop. The moon rose and cast a silvery light over the fields.

On and on they rattled through villages and market towns.

After a while the toys began to feel very tired and blown about by the cold wind. They did not know where they were and no one seemed to notice them speeding along the road. They longed to be safe and warm indoors.

Dandy was wondering which way to go and
where they could stop, when they heard a strange

roaring noise. It was the sound of a big diesel
train coming nearer and nearer.

Then the little engine stopped with a terrific jolt beside a level-crossing gate.

The lights were on in the level-crossing keeper's house.

The toys could see a little girl looking out of a window, waiting to see the train go by. In the room behind her was a Christmas tree, covered with tinsel and pretty lights.

The little girl could scarcely believe her eyes when she saw the bent toy engine outside with Dandy, Kate and Tiny Teddy sitting on it.

She ran out into the night to make sure she wasn't dreaming.

And there she found the bedraggled doll and teddy bears and a battered toy engine.

The little girl picked them up one by one and carried them all indoors.

She tidied them up and played with them by the Christmas tree.

Although she had plenty of new toys, these were the ones she liked most of all.

Dandy, Kate and Tiny Teddy were happy in their new home. And when the little girl gave them rides round the house on the toy engine, they always remembered their exciting ride through the night.